Tough Topics

Tobacco

DISCARDED

Ana Deboo

Heinemann Library
Chicago, Illinois

Customer Service   888–454–2279

Visit our Web site at www.heinemannlibrary.com

Photo research by Erica Martin and Ginny Stroud-Lewis
Designed by Richard Parker and Q2A Creative
Printed and bound in China by South China Printing Company

11 10 09 08 07
10 9 8 7 6 5 4 3 2 1

Library of Congress Cataloging-in-Publication Data
Deboo, Ana.
 Tobacco / Ana Deboo.
  p. cm. -- (Tough topics)
 Includes bibliographical references and index.
 ISBN 978-1-4034-9738-3 (hc) -- ISBN 978-1-4034-9743-7 (pb)
 1. Smoking--Juvenile literature. 2. Tobacco use--Juvenile literature. I. Title.
 HV5733.D43 2007
 613.85--dc22
                        2007002776

Acknowledgments
The author and publisher are grateful to the following for permission to reproduce copyright material:
Alamy Images pp. **10** (oote boe), **12** (ACE STOCK LIMITED), **14** (Westend61/Manfred J. Bail), **15** (ACE STOCK LIMITED), **18** (Oso Medias), **20** (Gianni Muratore), **21** (vario images GmbH & Co.KG), **22** (Wm. Baker / GhostWorx Images), **23** (Realimage); Corbis pp. **8**, **17** (Buddy Mays), **25** (Robert Landau), **26**, **27**; Getty Images pp. **4** (Retrofile/George Marks), **5** (Photodisc), **6** (Photodisc), **7** (Photographer's Choice/Garry Gay), **19** (Stone/John Millar), **29**; The Kobal Collection pp. **9**, **24**; Science Photo Library pp. **11** (PASCAL GOETGHELUCK), **13** (ALAIN DEX/PUBLIPHOTO DIFFUSION), **16** (Gusto), **28** (Doug Martin).

Cover photograph reproduced with permission of Corbis/Zuma/Marianna Day Massey.

Every effort has been made to contact copyright holders of any material reproduced in this book. Any omissions will be rectified in subsequent printings if notice is given to the publisher.

Contents

Some words are shown in bold, **like this**. You can find out what they mean by looking in the glossary.

Smoking Today

About 60 years ago, lots of people smoked tobacco. More than half the men in the United States smoked, and many women did, too. Since then we have learned how dangerous smoking is. Now far fewer people smoke.

◄ Smoking was very popular in the 1950s.

▲ In the United States today, about one person out of five smokes.

Cigarettes are the most common way people smoke tobacco. Smoking cigarettes can give you bad breath, stain your teeth, and make your clothes and hair smell. Smoking is also bad for your health.

What Is Tobacco?

▲ The United States is the fourth largest grower of tobacco in the world.

Tobacco is a plant that is grown in many parts of the world. It is related to plants that we eat, such as tomatoes, potatoes, and eggplants. It is also related to plants that contain poison.

Tobacco leaves are dried and used to make cigarettes, cigars, pipe tobacco, chewing tobacco, and **snuff**. All forms of tobacco contain a **drug** called **nicotine**.

◄ Many tobacco products are smoked.

Cigar

Tobacco's History

The first tobacco plants grew wild in the Americas. When Christopher Columbus arrived there in 1492, he saw how important tobacco was to the native people. European sailors tried tobacco, and its use quickly spread throughout the world.

◄ Native Americans smoked tobacco in some religious ceremonies.

◄ Early Hollywood stars often smoked in movies.

At first tobacco was too expensive for most people to buy. Then in the 1880s, a machine was invented that made cigarettes by the thousands. Suddenly many people could afford to buy cigarettes. By the 1950s, smoking was common in many parts of the world.

9

What Happens When You Use Tobacco?

When someone uses tobacco, **nicotine** quickly enters the bloodstream. Soon it reaches the brain, where it causes special **chemicals** to be released.

▲Smoking can damage your sense of smell.

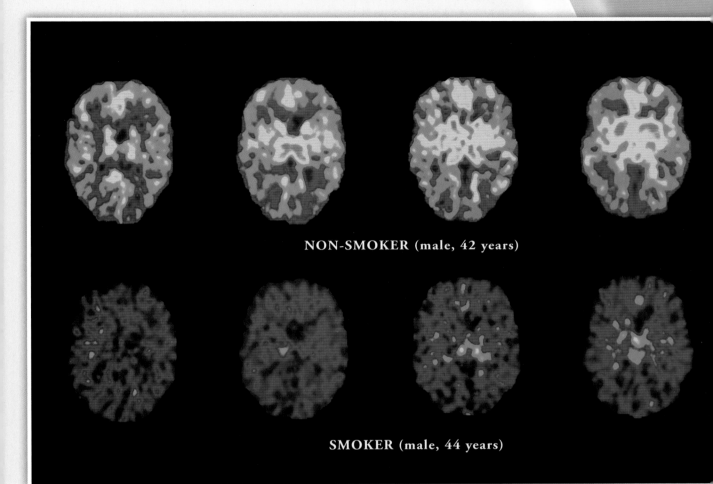

NON-SMOKER (male, 42 years)

SMOKER (male, 44 years)

▲ Smoking changes brain activity over time.

When nicotine sets these chemicals loose, they change the way the smoker feels. The smoker may feel more relaxed.

Tobacco Addiction

◄ Smoking irritates the lungs and can make a person cough.

Many people do not like smoking the first time they try it. It can make them feel dizzy or sick. But **nicotine** is **addictive**. It makes people feel as if they cannot live without it.

At first, nicotine can make people feel good. When these feelings begin to fade, people smoke more to bring them back. Over time, smokers get used to nicotine and have to smoke more often for it to **affect** them.

▲Smokers may feel sick when the nicotine level in the their body drops.

What Is Harmful About Tobacco?

◄ Cigarette smoke releases a harmful chemical that is also used in rat poison.

Nicotine makes people keep using tobacco, which contains other harmful **chemicals**. One of the most harmful chemicals in tobacco is called benzene. It can cause cancer.

▲ Carbon monoxide gas is also given off by cars. It can be deadly in large amounts.

Tobacco smoke contains carbon monoxide, a dangerous gas. It is **absorbed** into the blood and takes up space that carries oxygen. This means smokers cannot breathe as well as they should. Their lungs and heart have to work harder and can be damaged.

Another harmful material in cigarettes is **tar**, the burned particles (pieces) in tobacco smoke. When smokers **inhale**, these particles go deep into their lungs and stick there. Tar can make it harder for smokers to breathe.

◄ Tar can cause diseases such as lung cancer and **emphysema**.

▶People who chew tobacco have high rates of mouth cancers, gum disease, and dental problems.

Some people think chewing tobacco is safe because they do not inhale smoke when they use it. They do avoid **tar** and **carbon monoxide**, but the other **chemicals** in tobacco still get into the body.

How Does Smoking Affect Other People?

◄ Smoking risks the health of everyone around you.

For a long time, smoking was considered a risk adults took for themselves. Now it is known that people around smokers breathe in the same harmful substances. This is called **passive smoking**.

Passive smokers have a greater risk of lung and heart disease than people who do not live with smoke around them. Children are more likely to have lung problems such as **asthma** and **bronchitis** if they live with smokers.

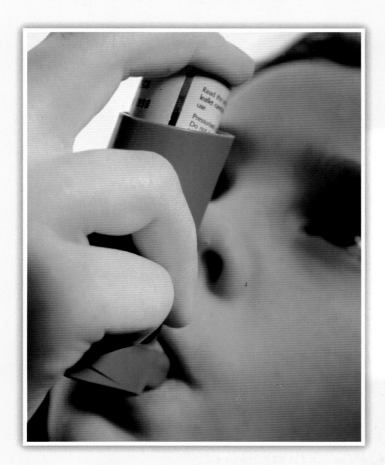

◄ People with asthma must sometimes use an inhaler to help them breathe.

Smoking and the Law

Many states do not allow smoking in public places, such as offices, stores, and restaurants. Smoking is also not allowed on airplanes in the United States.

▲ Workers who are **addicted** to cigarettes have to take breaks to smoke outside.

▲ Smoking remains popular even though people know it is not good for them.

Selling tobacco products to young people is illegal. However, these laws are not always obeyed. That often leaves it up to young people to decide for themselves what is the smart thing to do.

Why Do Kids Smoke?

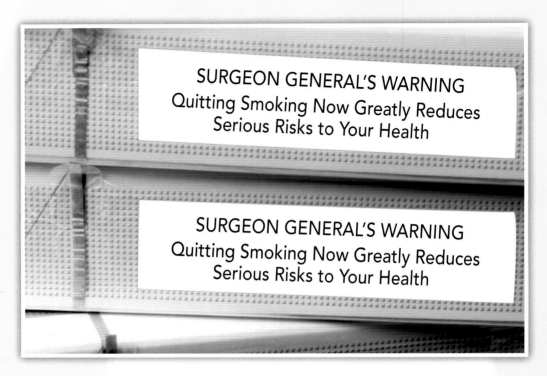

SURGEON GENERAL'S WARNING
Quitting Smoking Now Greatly Reduces
Serious Risks to Your Health

SURGEON GENERAL'S WARNING
Quitting Smoking Now Greatly Reduces
Serious Risks to Your Health

▲ Tobacco companies must include a health warning on cigarette packages.

Most people who smoke know that it can cause serious health problems. Still, a lot of young people try cigarettes and then become **addicted**.

Some young people start smoking because their friends do it. Some see family members smoking and want to know what it is like. Others may feel it helps them relax.

▶Young people may smoke because they think it makes them look older.

Tobacco Companies

Tobacco companies know that smoking is dangerous. However, if they do not get young people to start smoking, the companies will eventually lose all their customers. Some tobacco companies try to make smoking look appealing to young people.

◄ The "Marlboro man" has been used to sell Marlboro cigarettes since 1955.

◄ Johnny Depp played a character who smoked on the TV show *21 Jump Street*.

The U.S. government banned television advertisements for cigarettes in 1970. After that, cigarette companies encouraged the creators of television shows to use characters who smoke. That way, people would see actors smoking and may want to start, too.

Trying to Quit

◄ Few athletes smoke. They need strong, healthy lungs to perform well.

The sooner someone quits smoking, the better. The heart and lungs begin to **heal** over time. However, many people try to quit several times before they succeed. It is important to keep trying.

Some people try to quit by first cutting down on the number of cigarettes they smoke each day. Smoking fewer cigarettes usually makes people **inhale** more deeply with each puff. This can be just as bad as smoking more cigarettes without inhaling as hard.

◄ Smoking fewer cigarettes does not always lessen the health risks.

Help with Quitting

Quitting smoking can be difficult, but there are ways to get help. Special products that contain safe amounts of **nicotine** can help smokers quit. These include chewing gum and patches that are stuck onto the skin.

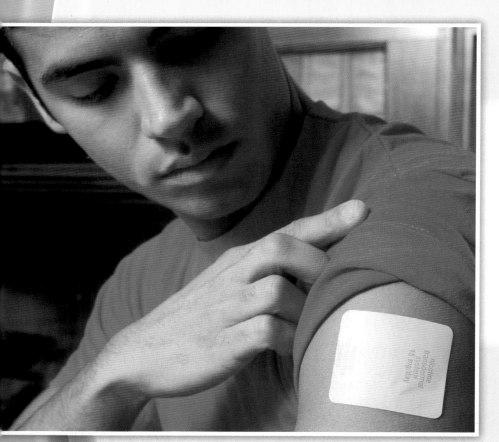

◄ Patches give smokers the nicotine they need to help them quit smoking.

▶Some cities have special days to remind people not to smoke.

Friends, family, and special organizations can help people who are struggling to quit smoking. Good places to look for information include the American Legacy Foundation and the Foundation for a Smoke-Free America.

Glossary

affect change

absorb soak in

addictive make a person feel as if they cannot live without it

asthma disease that can cause difficulty breathing

bronchitis swelling in the lungs that can cause breathing problems and severe coughing

carbon monoxide poisonous gas that is often created when something burns

chemical matter that can be created by or is used in scientific processes

drug something that is taken to change how the brain or body works

emphysema lung disease that can cause difficulty breathing and an infection in the lungs

flammable able to catch fire

heal get better

inhale breathe in

nicotine addictive chemical in tobacco products

passive smoking inhaling the smoke from other people's cigarettes

snuff tobacco product that is inhaled through the nose

tar small pieces of solid matter that make up cigarette smoke

Find Out More

Books to Read

Graves, Bonnie. *Tobacco Use.* Mankato, MN: Capstone, 2000.

Haughton, Emma. *A Right to Smoke?* New York: Franklin Watts, 1996.

Winters, Adam. *Tobacco and Your Mouth.* New York: Rosen, 2000.

Web Sites

- The American Legacy Foundation (www.americanlegacy.org) is dedicated to helping young people reject tobacco.

- The American Lung Association Web site is at www.lungusa.org.

- The Center for Disease Control has a special section on their Web site called Tips 4 Youth (www.cdc.gov/tobacco/tips4youth.htm).

Facts About Tobacco

- **Nicotine** is named after Jean Nicot, who lived in the 1500s in France. He thought that tobacco would turn out to be a useful medicine.

- Many house fires are started when a smoker puts a lit cigarette too close to something **flammable**. Forest fires can be started when people throw burning cigarettes into dry grass.

- In the United States, about 1,200 deaths a day are caused by the effects of cigarette smoking.

Index

D **D**

Tough Topics
Tobacco

- **What is nicotine?**
- **What are common tobacco products?**
- **How does smoking cigarettes harm the body?**

Books in the **Tough Topics** series offer a first introduction to difficult issues that many young people face. Each book gives straightforward information about the subject, answering common questions students may have to help them make informed decisions.

Read **Tobacco** to learn about tobacco use in history and today. Get the facts on tobacco's health risks, nicotine addiction, and ways to get help when trying to quit smoking.

Titles in the series:
Alcohol
Death
Divorce and Separation
Drugs
Illness
Moving
Safety Around the House
Tobacco

About the Author:
Ana Deboo is an editor and writer who lives on Vashon Island, Washington.

Book Consultant:
Gillian Dowley McNamee, Ph.D., is a professor of child development and director of teacher education at Erikson Institute in Chicago. She works closely with early childhood teacher candidates and with teachers in schools.

ISBN-13: 978-1-4034-9743-7
ISBN-10: 1-4034-9743-5

Heinemann Raintree

heinemannraintree.com

IN CANADA

90000

9 781403 497437

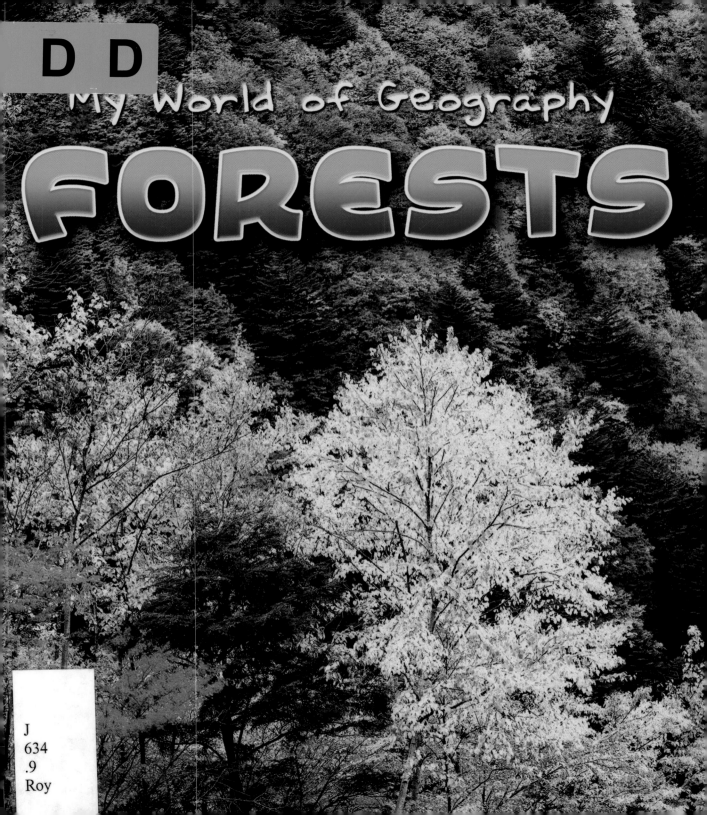

My World of Geography

FORESTS

© 2005 Heinemann Library
a division of Reed Elsevier Inc.
Chicago, Illinois

Customer Service 888-454-2279
Visit our website at www.heinemannlibrary.com

Design: Ron Kamen and Celia Jones
Illustrations: Barry Atkinson (pp. 28–29), Jo Brooker (p. 13), Jeff Edwards (p. 5)
Photo Research: Rebecca Sodergren, Melissa Allison, and Debra Weatherley
Originated by Ambassador Litho
Printed and bound in China by South China Printing

09 08 07 06 05
10 9 8 7 6 5 4 3 2 1

**Library of Congress
Cataloging-in-Publication Data**

Royston, Angela.
  Forests / Angela Royston.
     p. cm. – (My world of geography)
  Includes bibliographical references and index.
  ISBN 1-4034-5589-9 (HC), 1-4034-5598-8 (Pbk)
  1. Forests and forestry–Juvenile literature.
     I. Title. II. Series.
  SD376.R68 2005
  634.9–dc22
                                2004004108

Acknowledgments
The author and publisher are grateful to the following for permission to reproduce copyright material:
pp. 4, 6, 7, 8, 9, 11, 14, 16, 17 (James Marshall), 19 (Lynda Richardson), 20, 21 (Enzo & Paolo Ragazzini), 26 (Dave Houser), 27 (Wolfgang Kaehler) Corbis; p. 10 Ardea/Adrian Warren; pp. 12 (Robert Harding Picture Library/D. Hughes), 25 (Worldwide Picture Library/Sue Cunningham) Alamy Images; pp. 15 (Geoff Tompkinson), 18 (Maximillian Stock Ltd.), 22 (Colin Cuthbert) Science Photo Library; p. 23 (Trevor Clifford) Harcourt Education Ltd.; p. 24 Getty Images/Photodisc.

Cover photograph reproduced with permission of Corbis.

Every effort has been made to contact copyright holders of any material reproduced in this book. Any omissions will be rectified in subsequent printings if notice is given to the publisher.

Contents

Some words are shown in bold, **like this.** You can find out what they mean by looking in the glossary.

What Is a Forest?

A forest is an area of land where lots of trees grow. **Ferns, mosses,** and other plants grow there, too. Some forests are very large.

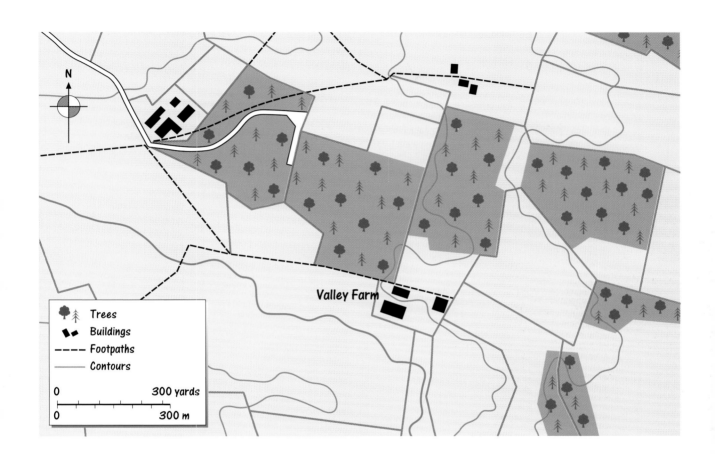

This map shows a small forest. The
forest is colored green and is covered
with small pictures of trees.

Coniferous Forests

Coniferous forests are forests where mainly pine and fir trees grow. These trees have **cones** and needles instead of leaves. Coniferous trees grow well in cold countries.

This pinecone is growing in a coniferous forest.

Huge coniferous forests cover the land near the **Arctic Circle.** Beavers, bears, wolves, and **caribou** live in coniferous forests in northern Asia, Europe, and North America.

This is a caribou in northern Canada.

Deciduous Forests

Deciduous forests have trees with broad, flat leaves. Deciduous trees grow well in countries that are not very hot in summer and not very cold in winter.

In the fall the green leaves on deciduous trees change to yellow, red, or brown. Then the leaves fall off the trees. The trees are bare all winter. New leaves grow on the trees in spring.

Tropical Forests

Tropical forests grow in hot lands. The trees that grow in these areas have broad, green leaves all year long.

This tropical forest has a river running through it.

Rain forests are very wet because
they get rain nearly every day.
The weather is always wet and hot—
just right for many kinds of plants
to grow.

11

Traveling in Forests

In some places, the easiest way to travel through a thick forest is by boat along a river. In other places, people build roads through the forest to make traveling easier.

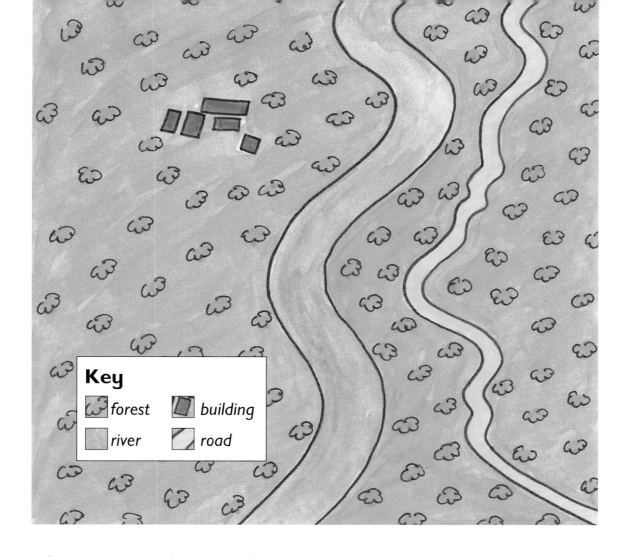

This map shows the same part of a forest as the photograph on page 12. The forest has a road and river running through it. You could draw a map like this.

Using Coniferous Trees

People cut down trees so they can use the wood. Wood from **coniferous** trees is cut into pieces. It is used to build the frames of houses, as well as doors and furniture.

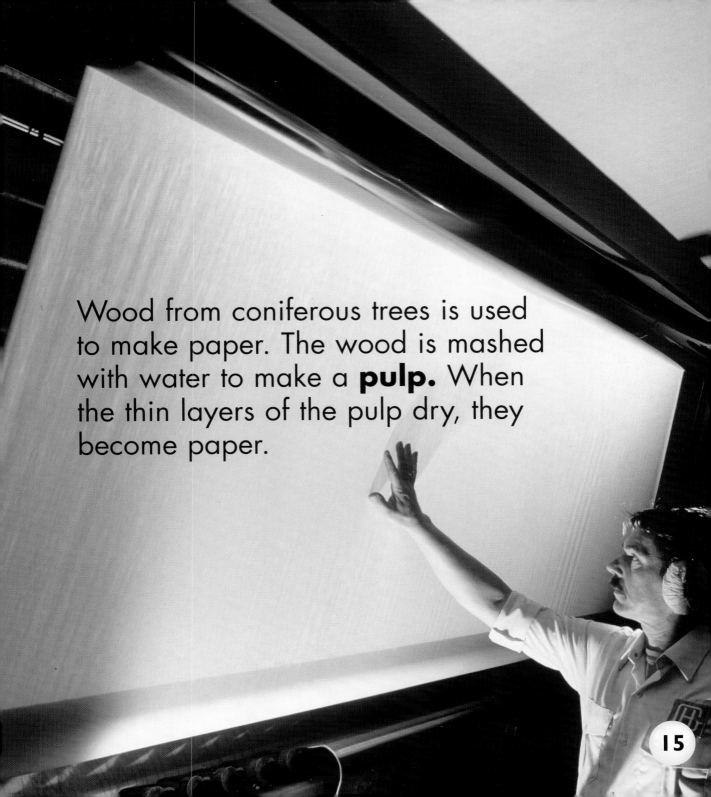

Wood from coniferous trees is used to make paper. The wood is mashed with water to make a **pulp.** When the thin layers of the pulp dry, they become paper.

Using Deciduous Trees

The wood from some **deciduous** trees is strong and hard. It is used to make things like floors and furniture.

This wooden furniture is made of oak.

These buckets are being used to collect syrup dripping from maple trees.

Some trees are useful for more than just wood. Maple syrup is a sugary juice that drips from the wood of some maple trees. Cork comes from the bark of a cork oak.

Using Tropical Trees

There are more kinds of plants and animals in **tropical** forests than anywhere else on Earth. Many of the nuts and fruits that we eat come from tropical forests.

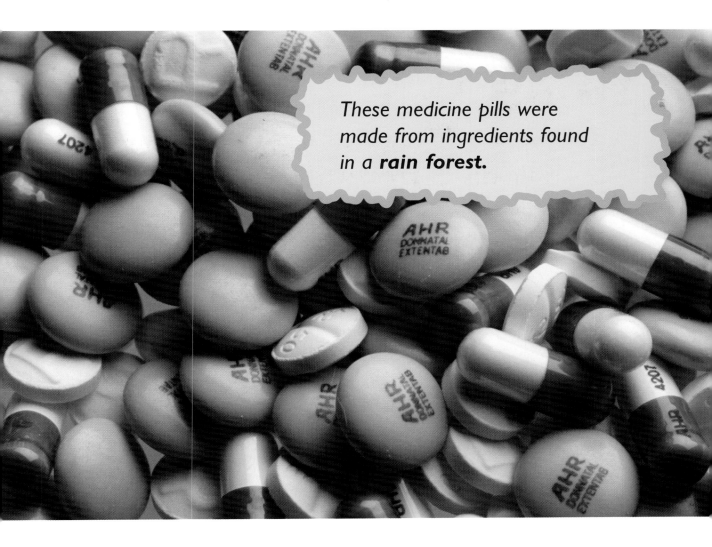

*These medicine pills were made from ingredients found in a **rain forest**.*

Creams, **lotions,** and **medicines** can be made from forest plants. Scientists think that there are many useful forest plants that have not been discovered yet.

Farming Forest Land

Hundreds of years ago, much of the land in the United States was covered by forests. Many large forests were cut down so people could farm the land.

Many **tropical** forests have been cut down and **crops** planted instead. These crops include **rubber,** coffee, and cocoa.

These coffee plants have been grown in place of a **rain forest** in Colombia, a country in South America.

21

Replanting Trees

Some forests are specially planted to provide wood for **timber** and paper. Whenever a tree is cut down in one of these forests, a new tree is planted.

Many books are printed on paper
from replanted trees. The trees in
replanted forests are usually
coniferous trees that grow quickly.
Trees in **tropical** and **deciduous**
forests take many years to grow.

Enjoying the Forests

Forests are peaceful places to be. Many people visit forests to walk among the trees. Other people go to watch the birds and other animals that live there.

Tourists visit the Amazon **rain forest** in South America. They travel through part of the forest by boat. Some people live in this forest.

Protecting the Forests

Rain forest trees like mahogany and teak are cut down because their wood is very valuable. The wood is sold in Europe and North America.

This worker in Thailand is making furniture from teak wood.

When rain forest trees are cut down, the rain washes away the soil. Without soil, nothing else can grow there. If people stop buying wood from rain forests, fewer trees will be cut down.

Different Forest Trees

Every kind of tree has a particular shape of leaf. Here are the leaves and needles of a few **deciduous** trees, **coniferous** trees, and **tropical rain forest** trees.

camphor

teak

Rain forest trees

Rain forest trees are always green. They lose some leaves and grow new ones all year long. Most rain forest trees have long trunks with leaves and flowers far above the ground where there is more light.

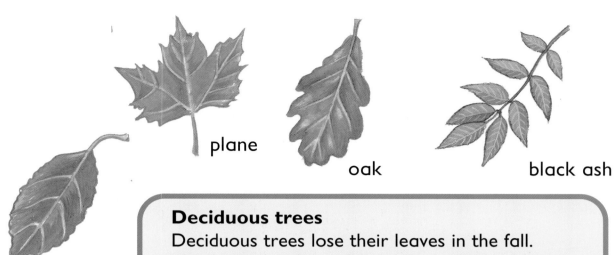

plane

oak

black ash

apple

Deciduous trees
Deciduous trees lose their leaves in the fall.
At the same time, new buds form that contain
tiny leaves and flowers that will grow the
following spring.

pine

spruce

fir

Scotch pine

cedar

Conifer Trees
Conifer trees are sometimes called evergreen
because most of them have needles all year long.
The world's tallest trees (redwoods) and oldest
trees (bristlecone pines) are conifers.

Glossary

Arctic Circle cold far north of Earth

caribou another name for reindeer

cone part of some trees, such as firs, pines, and cedars, that produces seeds

coniferous producing cones instead of flowers and fruit

contour line on a map that shows how high a place is

crop plant grown for food

deciduous losing leaves at a particular time of year, usually in the fall

fern plant with feathery leaves and no flowers

lotion thick liquid that is rubbed into the skin

medicine something that helps make you feel better when you are sick

moss small, green plant with tiny leaves

pulp soft, wet mixture of tiny pieces of wood and water

rain forest forest that grows in places that are wet all year long

rubber stretchy material that does not let air or water pass through it

timber lengths of wood cut from tree trunks

tourist person who visits a place on vacation

tropical coming from hot, wet places on or near the Equator

More Books to Read

Ashwell, Miranda, and Andy Owen. *Forests.* Chicago: Heinemann Library, 1998.

Galko, Francine. *Forest Animals.* Chicago: Heinemann Library, 2003.

Galko, Francine. *Rain Forest Animals.* Chicago: Heinemann Library, 2003.

Kalman, Bobbie, and Kathryn Smithyman. *What Is a Forest?* New York: Crabtree Publishing, 2002.

Klingel, Cynthia Fitterer. *Forests.* Chanhassen, Minn.: Child's World, 2001.

Loughran, Donna. *Living in the Forest.* Danbury, Conn.: Scholastic Library, 2003.

Williams, Judith. *Exploring the Rain Forest Treetops with a Scientist.* Berkeley Heights, N.J: Enslow Publishers, 2004.

Index